# Caycee's Cave

## ~ An Irish Tale ~

by

Holly K. Szurpicki

*Caycee's Cave – An Irish Tale*
Copyright © 2017—Holly K. Szurpicki

ISBN    978-0-9992323-0-9

Published by Szurpicki Productions
Illustrations by Derek Stewart
Text Design by Lisa Simpson

Library of Congress Control Number: 2017911291

# Dedication

I am thankful for my family who encourage me daily, especially my two children, Jonathon and Colleen. I am thankful for my beautiful mom who resides in heaven and is dearly missed. I am blessed to be loved by an amazing husband and a divine God. For those who are fighting a battle, continue to be strong and know you are a **"Warrior-right-on,"** which means *an individual who remains faithful to fight in any situation, knowing that their inner strength comes from within."* *(Nobel Reszen)*

# Table of Contents

# Introduction

Living on an island can be quite an adventure, especially if you have a spunky Irish sister and a one-of-a-kind sheep dog to share it with.

Evolone Hills is mountainous and vast and can only be reached by boat. On the far side of the island there is a mystical dwelling which no one dare enter, a place where legend speaks of a horrible creature, a golden dragon, who hunts the oceans relentlessly day and night searching to devour anything that comes in its path. No one pays attention to legends and tales these days anyway, or do they?

Yipson and Caycee daringly journey beyond the arch stones to discover a tale once hidden, now divinely unfolding and tell of a story long ago.

Life for the Minors was not easy. Faith, determination and being a family, the impossible can become the possible. Legends are truly neat and you, my dearest friend, are in for a fantastic treat!

Chapter 1

# Euglone Hills

# Evalone Hills

O h, how I wish I was back in my humble home reclining in my leather chair while in front of my stone hearth as the glow from the orange embers radiate off my face and warm my heart. Sounds sappy, doesn't it? I'd be smelling a cast iron pot filled full of potato dumplings oozing bubbles jam-packed with fragrant spices such as nutmeg and cinnamon. Instead, I lean against a cold, jagged rock on the highest peak of ol' Mountain Blew. The wind is beating my face and ruffling my nose hairs.

Never you mind. I'm wrapped like a burrito in an itchy wool blanket my mum made for me when I was just a boy. In my pocket is a taste of home—sourdough bread stuffed with raspberry curd nestled in a moist ginger muffin. `Tis an Irish man's delight! We're toasty warm. Isn't that right, Patsy Rose? You're a good ol' girl, aren't yaw! She loves it when my beard tickles the top of her head. She needs no blanket; her black matted fur keeps her body quite warm.

We've been visiting this majestic place for about sixty years. The enchanted fields of lavender beckon us to climb this sacred mountain. It's grand here; it is where I call my home. It is the island of Evolone Hills. The people settled here long ago. Some are Irish and English and some are Scottish folk. This isn't the life for everyone. It's a remote place, and only sea men can reach this island.

Ships sail in and out of the Hills providing goods and services for many folks. These seas bring unexpected visitors and traders. It's the most welcome place to fill your belly and get a good night's rest from the treacherous sea and creatures so strange they would blow your mind. Strange folk live in the valleys and in the mountains. Strange, as in peculiarly odd.

Speaking of peculiar is a man by the name of Mr. Stickel. Despite his solidarity, he enjoys our company only from a distance. He's a hermit. Lanky in stature with hair like a black bear and ears like saucers. He settled here as a young lad, never married and he is a fierce gardener.

Each year our town celebrates the harvest. It's a bountiful time filled with goodness! Good ol' Mr. Stickel is known for growing the largest zucchini with ginormous measurements. It hurts my melon just talking about it, but it could feed a small village weighing in at a whopping 250 pounds. Now, that's a zucchini, dare I say!

His home is modest and humble, made of grass and a tin can chimney. He may not be good-looking, but who am I to say anything about his homely looks? I have long hair and prefer to braid it. It stays out of my eyes that way! It's silver now, but once flowed as the color of strawberry blond.

Did I mention I have an overbite?  I find it rather useful when the time comes for opening cans or biting into a spoon filled with beefy meaty stew. However, it's awful when you're trying to slurp a bowl of bubbly onion soup! I'd come prepared if I were you with extra napkins in your pockets.

I have only one sister and her name is Caycee. We look nothing alike. She's slender and tall with pale skin and piercing green eyes and overgrown hair like a Heather bush. I, on the other hand, am short and stubby.

Let's get back to the story, shall we? Mr. Stickel prefers to live at a distance from all humans. Not so long ago he faced an unwelcome visitor. Patsy Rose dashed towards a fattened squirrel feasting on the wheat in the field. I yelled for her, but she never listened. I couldn't see my girl. I knew she was in trouble, and I set my mind to find her. I charged fearlessly like an Irish knight through the thick bushes. The forest is not a forgiving place; it is full of thorns and nasty prickled branches resembling hands. They will scrape and cut your skin. The deeper I pushed through, the thicker the bushes became. They forced me to stop dead in my Olivers. In case you didn't know, Olivers are brown leather boots which have a great tread for climbing. They are not very fashionable to look at, but they are rather functional. I suggest you buy a pair for traveling, especially if you are into climbing.

Two shadows appeared in front of me blocking the sun. The hair on my back stood to attention, and I was shivering something fierce. Afraid, trapped in the bushes with nowhere to go all while hearing the whimpers of Patsy, but I couldn't get to her. I heard a man's voice. "Your dog was running in my field. Care to explain?" I froze in fear as two large masses of skin appeared before me. "Brimley Blimmers!" I exclaimed. I had never seen such a sight before!

"Well, I'll be a horn snaggled snip dog on a boggle train. I didn't know you could have ears that big. I thought only elephants had them." Our eyes locked and I blundered, "Bricking snoopers, your ears are fairly large, Stickel man!" It was then I realized that I had a not so funny of a problem. First, it's never wise to blurt out something you're thinking. Secondly, when the person you are thinking about is standing directly in front of you. Thirdly, and you can't go anywhere because one false move and your bum will be filled with prickles. Certainly, this was extremely unwise of me.

Mr. Stickel was certainly not fond of humans, a vivacious hermit he was. I hoped he would have mercy on me and let me kindly retreat. Not likely, because above my head I heard a flapping sound. Curious, I thought it was a disturbed bird, but it was not a bird. It was Mr. Stickel hovering in mid-air directly over my head. Not only were his ears ginormous; they were like miniature propellers. Terrified, I screamed, "Oh, please don't fly into my nose!" Yes, that is what I thought!

My nose is big and many things have flown in my nostrils over the years like small birds, agitating flies and even a hummingbird once. On one occasion, I was sniffing a freshly baked biscuit, and a piece broke off and flew up my nostril. That gave me a sneeze not to be believed!

Now the hummingbird, well, that made it hard for me to sleep. My nose vibrated, and I was annoyed by the constant buzzing of the wings. I shook my head back and forth muttering and complaining about my unfortunate situation. Eventually the bird flew out my nose. I was so very grateful! Oh, I'm sorry, let me get back to the story. Pardon me, I am rambling on about my nose.

Frightened, I watched as Mr. Stickel tightly gripped her collar and her legs dangled over my head. Feeling helpless, I attempted to jump towards her, but I couldn't because of the thick bushes surrounding me. Eventually Mr. Stickel released her, and she plummeted to the ground. It was then that my ol' girl leaped into my arms, and she was one happy girl.

"Oh, Patsy girl, why did you take off?" She licked my face and her breath smelled awful. It was time to get back to home. I had my fill of this ol' mountain today. "Come on, girl." Patsy was a little slow in her old age, but she still manages to get along.

Now, let's see. Where was I? Ah yes, food, I am hungry now! I had all but forgotten a hearty pot of beefy stew was cooking at home. "We better get back home, Patsy Rose, before the coals burn out." There is nothing like settling in for the night with a warm belly while gazing out my living room window watching the stars light up the night sky.

Our pantry was always stocked, lacking nothing. In the morning we'd enjoy crispy, buttery, nutty cookies. Caycee and I devoured them, but not without drinking a glass of creamy milk first. It was not uncommon for Mum to be tending to the farmstead while we gobbled our delectable delights!

There's always a job to do, and everyone pitched in to get the work done. Milking cows, feeding chickens, doing laundry, making breads and stocking berry jams, cleaning the barn, sweeping and folding. I could go on, but you get the idea. Caycee and I had just finished drinking our milk. Our tummies were full, and we were already sneaking around the kitchen, looking for afternoon snacks.

Caycee heard someone yelling from outside the house. She looked out the window. "Yipson, come see. Mum's running towards the house. Something must be wrong. It looks like she is carrying something, something rather large."

Abruptly the front door flung open. I was still in my nickers and terrified of what I saw. Patsy Rose was swaddled in her arms, with red blood on her. Frantically she yelled, "Yipson, get Dr. Rainton right now!" I saw the worry etched on her face. "Mum, what do I do?" Caycee cried. "Just stay here and keep Patsy comfortable; pet her head." Caycee bent down and gently caressed Patsy's head, massaging her ears and trying to calm her by offering soft words of encouragement while maintaining a gentle stroke of her hand. "My words seem to be getting better in my old age." "Yes, Mum,"

I whizzed past her to my bedroom, and there I put on my clothes. I was anxious to get outside immediately. I hopped on my yellow bicycle and peddled as fast as I could to reach the village. My heart pounded inside my chest. Over the years we had our share of surprises living on a farm, but nothing ever like this. It felt as though I was peddling forever until I reached the village and saw Dr. Rainton locking the door to the clinic. I yelled out to him. If only I had arrived a few minutes later, I would have missed him. Dr. Rainton sat on the rusty handlebars as I madly peddled us home. It was hard to see in front of me. The doctor wasn't a small man in stature, but rather wide and full.

Never underestimate someone with little legs. I was fierce that day. We arrived at the house, and Dr. Rainton examined her. Caycee looked concerned, and I noticed her nose was sniffling. She had been crying since I left. It was hard for her to see the family pet in such pain.

It appeared she was kicked by a farm horse, and her hind leg was broken. Her bones were severely shattered and could not be repaired. There's no telling what farm horses will do to other animals. Sometimes they can be the kindest of animals, and other times not so much! Work horses are extremely ornery, and they certainly don't like pesky old dogs bothering them. My father warned us all the time to stay clear of them, but our dog tended to ignore instructions.

Dr. Rainton said, "One, you could put her down; or two, she will lose her hind leg. Now, if I remove her hind leg, she will be a bit slower but she will live." There was no hesitation from Mum. "So be it. Take her hind leg." Caycee and I left the house. It was too much for two children to bear. After all, Patsy Rose was not just a pet. She was part of the family. I was glad my mum was faced with this decision, because if my father was home he would have shot her.

My father was a farmer and a woodworker, and he was all about business. He made it a point to never have any feelings when it came to animals on our farm, but Mum felt the opposite. She was kind at heart just like my sister Caycee. She cared for all kinds of animals.

It took only a few weeks, and Patsy Rose eventually began to hobble around the house. Father carved a wooden leg for her from an old oak tree and attached a leather brace to her neck and side. It was secure. She whined and huffed at first, but in no time at all she took to it. She ran faster than she did before.

*"There are times when we huff and puff,*
*whine and cry and spiffily snuff,*
*only to discover things were not*
*as extreme as they seemed."*
(Nobel Reszen)

CHAPTER 2

# It's Not Always Easy

# It's Not Always Easy

I have found stories and tales are quite different. Stories are filled with imagination and can have real people as characters in them, while tales are filled with characters and enchantment few people truly understand. I cherish my stories, and over the years I have built quite a collection of literary works to enjoy. Glancing at my wooden bookshelf, which could use some minor repairs, there's not much space anymore from years of collecting. I have a few select novels on top where the dust mites collect.

I probably should add some more wood to my fireplace as there is a chill in the air. As the darkness settles in, I am reminded that in life there can be dark times—times your soul is miserable. I have learned many things along the pathway of this life. I wish I could tell you how easy it has been or how easy it will be. Honestly, there are no shortcuts to growing older and wiser in this short life. Time for some is their worst enemy, but time for me showed me who I truly am.

My sister enjoyed reading, but she did not love to read when she was younger. It became a source of contention within our house. Mum asked that she read to increase her vocabulary. "Mum, not another book; I just finished one," Caycee yelled. "Nonsense! You will read until you learn to love it!" "What if I don't love it? I mean, what if I never love it? This just isn't fair. Why do we read anyway?" disgruntled as she spoke. "I want to be outside playing in the fields, listening to the crickets, chasing butterflies and finding treasures in the ocean."

Caycee, with crossed arms swayed back and forth in bed. "When I get older, I will become an author and write books myself. I mean, how hard can it be to write a novel anyway? I will write about adventure and drama and mystery. I am tired of reading chapter after chapter full of nothing but words boring me to death! How long does it take to explain something, really?"

Mum snickered as she overheard her murmuring from the living room. She continued to knit a multicolored afghan. Mum loves Caycee's spirit! My sister was witty and wise even though she was only eight years of age. Speaking of good books in my hand, I hold a special one. It's not a book filled with illustrations or mere pictures, but it contains literary treasures and shimmering gold. Legend says that in the heart of a child is the purest gold of all.

The ocean is alive in this book, along with the crashing of the waves. If you listen intently, you can hear it roar. If you believe in the visibility of this tale, you may even smell the saltiness of the water; but if you loathe tales and don't believe in imagination, all you will smell is stinky fish!

They say that dogs have a keen smell for adventure and imagination. They can see things mere humans cannot. Sometimes Patsy Rose barks at nothing, silly girl. One evening as I sat by the fire, I heard a faint knock at the door. Why is it that when I am most comfortable I must get up and answer the door? I glanced around my abode, and no one was there. Of course, I sat back down. Then I heard the knocking sound again. Gobbling snucklebees! I got up from my chair to answer the door. I thought it might be some pesky children roaming about the area seeking to irritate an old man. They sometimes like to play pranks by knocking on the door and then running away.

Dogs are not the only ones who involve themselves in shenanigans. Knock, Knock. This time I realized the knocking sound was coming from the kitchen under the sink. I strolled over to the sink and noticed a piece of fur moving up and down the cabinet. Curious, I opened the cabinet door and Patsy came barreling out, panting and wagging her tail in excitement. I discovered she was not alone under the sink. A wee mouse scurried away burrowing into a crack in the wall which I was meaning to fix, but never got around to it.

Patsy sat down right in front of the hole, wagging her tail and waiting for her friend to return. I could hear the critter "chitter chatter" behind the wall. There was no way that mouse was coming out of the wall while she was there. After all the chasing in such a confined space, she was thirsty. When Patsy wanted water, she brought me her dish and threw it at my feet. That was my sign to fill her up!

She was unlike other dogs. Nothing stopped her from enjoying adventure. She was a treasure seeker and a nose sniffer. She could smell anything for miles. Anytime she got the chance, she darted to the fields in search of mice and other small rodents. It was hard to see her sometimes because she blended in well in the tall grass. We have had our share of mice, especially in the winter season.

*"Animals find adventure*
*in places mere humans tend not to look;*
*however, humans find adventures*
*reading a clever book."*
(Nobel Reszen)

Chapter 3

# The Evil Rule

# The Evil Rule

It was a different time back when I was a young lad. Our family lived under the reign of an evil ruler. You must remember that not all royalty is inherently evil. The king was not always heartless, and at one time he was quite generous and was liked by many.

He had sorrow befall him when his son died unexpectedly from a horrible virus. It was then that his heart became dark and his thoughts twisted within him. His soul filled with deep sadness, greed overcame him and he treated others cruelly.

It was the four of us—Mum, Father, Caycee and me—and we lived below the castle in a tiny household off a winding, heavily wooded pathway! The castle was built into a mountain and was under constant construction and renovation. The wind from the ocean wreaked havoc on the mountain landscape. The king summoned stone workers to expand the staircase around the castle. He wanted to be able to walk around the whole castle anytime he wished.

The views were spectacular for royalty, but not for his peasant servants, for all they had was mud and rotted vegetation surrounding them. Their view was obstructed by tree roots growing in a muddy mosquito-infested bog. The people who served him below dealt with horrible living conditions, and he didn't care. The king's heart was hardened and bitterness was the soul of his song.

I had only been inside the castle a few times as a little boy. I went along with my father when he was working, and I watched as skilled artists painted watercolor murals on the ceilings. Large oil paintings adorned the walls, and every beam was painted in fourteen carat gold. Everything was well appointed from red carpeting to the beautiful tapestries and marble tiled floors. Inside the king's quarters were hidden rooms with fake wooden walls, golden goblets and crystal plates. The soft glow from the lighted chandelier exposed a cluster of deer antlers, beveled glass doors and a very large fireplace, providing quite the ambiance.

A master suite was made specifically for the queen. An all glass sunroom was filled with exotic plants and decadent velvet furnishings. Greenery ropes hung from the ceiling. It was there where the queen practiced vine swinging. She was agile swinging almost like a monkey, but more graceful.

King Ballot lived lavishly, gorging himself from others' provision. The king continually beat them down with harsh words and hurt them by dishonoring them and using them for his own personal gain. King Ballot afflicted children by eating their only food supply, causing them to nearly starve to death. They didn't starve to death, but they did become ill because of dehydration and lack of nutrition for their bones. He seized their food to fill his own stomach. He slew great giants of the land because they would not partake in his selfish, gluttonous life.

They did not consider his earthly rule favorable, but they revered a Heavenly King of great worth. The king had no regard for those who lived below his castle. He allowed murky water from the castle sewer system to trickle onto those below. The people prayed for fresh rainwater to pour down and clean the area in which they lived and rid them from such filth.

Viciously, he mistreated women, demanding they slave over him, giving him anything he so selfishly desired. Once a month they were forced to bathe him and groom his long-ratted hair. His robe stunk and smelled like body odor, a combination of rotted vegetables and old vinegar. If that wasn't bad enough, they were forced to trim his fungal-ridden toenails. Nasty, slimy, sticky skin collected in between his toes; and he required them to fish it out with their fingers.

While I am telling you this story, I thought about having a dill pickle, but merely talking about this beasty king has caused me to rethink my snacking plan. I think I'll wait for a bit.

The king wanted his kingdom to be larger than all the other kingdoms. The men worked long hours, they missed their families and they were tired and downtrodden. Their bodies broke down from years of working. They had aching hands, backs and sore feet. Sometimes they rested, but it was only because they fell over on the ground from complete and utter exhaustion.

King Ballot felt his power was all they needed to fill their souls. He reveled in watching others suffer, for it made him feel good about himself. He felt he was privileged, and those beneath him were not.

His queen, however, was breathtakingly beautiful to behold. She had a light about her, a glow almost like an angel. Her long, flowing red hair fell to her hips, and she wore mirrored glasses with golden rims which showcased her bluish green eyes perfectly. She had a smile that could light the stars, and dimples gently caressing the sides of each cheek.

The queen conformed daily to her husband's demands, giving him every wish he desired. At least that is what she made him think she did. There was a side of Queen Gildiah that the king did not know about nor did his servants speak of it—a kind side, a gentle side, a humbleness which was abnormal for most royalty.

In the night hours, she slipped past the king's guards secretly by swinging from a tree vine to the forest below them. She wore a red and gold belted cape which covered her gorgeous locks of shimmering red hair. In her hand was a basket filled with goodies made especially for the children the king unjustly starved. On each doorstep, she gingerly left a small portion of bread or a tea cake and a tiny white and red wildflower. Then she would sneak back to the castle and quietly lay beside the king as he was snoring.

Daily the king and queen received bountiful baskets filled with freshly packaged produce and root vegetables from their slaves below: leeks, potatoes, carrots, beets and onions wrapped in spices; freshly baked breads and decadent desserts.

The people obeyed them because King Nissi said, "Be obedient to all authority on earth." Even under dark rule and utter despicable living conditions, they always managed to handle their dark situation with grace. Before Mum would give them our share, she would skillfully prepare a bowl of soup for each of us; and with a gracious smile on her face Mum always thought of others, and Caycee was just like her. I heard the saying, "A daughter is a mirror to her mum," or something like that!

Both of our parents worked hard. Father made a living being an expert carpenter. He was summoned by the king to carve detailed pieces for his castle and surrounding servant quarters. Wooden rose and ivy were his specialty, and the queen adored his one-of-a-kind furniture. Of course, this made the king very envious at times, for he had not one talent in his bones.

The king was never satisfied, and neither were his demands. His appetite for greed was exhausting and burdensome. Under great persecution, Father worked without complaint. As a courtesy, the king's men allowed Father to keep scraps of wood. They told him it was because he was admirable and trustworthy. Truthfully, they didn't want to clean up the scraps; they were lazy! What the king's men didn't know is that Father used these scraps to build a small wooden boat. He hid it in a room in an underground cave, and it was there he constructed, designed and built it. Father concealed it by gathering moss he found, and he used fishing nets to make the covering.

In the evenings as our father tucked us into a nice cozy bed, he would tell a tale and end his story with this song. *"One day when the winds are blowin' and the moon's light is showin', we'll be knowin', freedom is ours. We'll be lights on the ocean, free from commotion and we'll hold tight to each other knowin', freedom is ours."* "It's a promise," he said as he kissed us both on the cheek and said good-night. He blew out the candle beside our beds, and I sniffed the familiar smell of burnt wax and smoke. Of course, it made me sneeze something awful.

*"No matter how things unpleasantly arrange,
in a moment they can swiftly change."*
(Nobel Reszen)

CHAPTER 4

# The Escape

# The Escape

For a long time, my father and mum desperately wished for our family to be free from the tyranny of the wicked king. They dreamed of one day living in peace with no fear, and so did Caycee and I; we dreamed with them.

Each Sunday after the collection for the king, the people would celebrate for two days. It was a feast which took place. There was dancing, baking, cooking, laughing, fireworks and cliff jumping. There was no fear in the young men of the village. They would climb to the tallest cliff, with a crowd of voices egging them on. Yelling JUMP, JUMP, cheering, they would plummet into the water beneath them.

King Ballot had an underwater creature named Enstora. From his vantage point high above the ocean, the scenery was clear; and he could see his beast shadowing the rocks below. She was a treacherous beast, living in a dark, gloomy dungeon deep under the chilling sea. Enstora scurried across the water with long, scaly tentacles resembling a slithering snake. Her tail held hundreds of feathers with eyes covering each of them. Whenever the king was present, the waters surrounding her would turn black as night.

The king summoned his guards to release her into the water, even though the boys in the swamps below were jumping into the water. He didn't care. He wanted to scare them, and he used the underwater beast named Enstora to do it.

He would not feed her for days, hoping she would feed on unexpected visitors swimming in the area. But she had reserve fish hidden in her watery cave and would eat her fill. Enstora carried young swimmers on her back safely to the shore. She enjoyed jumping into the air like a humpback whale, performing quite a spectacular show. This made the king angry because he loathed kindness and refused to show kindness to others!

The evil King Ballot allowed a small window of festivities to commemorate in which they would celebrate his wealth and provision for the people. They made him believe that their celebration was because of his provision. In secret, they were thanking their Heavenly King who provided them with strength for daily living and the land by which their hands worked the soil and harvested for their families.

The people cooked continuously for two days creating culinary masterpieces in preparation for the thankful jubilee. The women and children seared seasoned turkey kabobs layered with apples and dried strawberry slices. They soaked apricot tree branches in water and roasted the kabobs over an open fire. The smell of the wood burning while cooking the meat created a savory aroma which caused me to slightly drool. Smelly cheeses were processed and turned daily. Cheese making was a skill, and they took it seriously. The process to make the cheeses was extensive but well worth the wait.

Typically, milk is carried by wooden buckets, then transferred into larger containers for sorting. Children are required to stir the milk with large wooden spoons until clumps of curds began to form by separating from the milk. Spices are added for a scrumptious yet savory flavor.

The women whip up dozens of pumpkin scones, each one hand dipped in a sugary maple glaze. Plum and chokecherry jams canned in green jars with red and white bows were added for decoration. The bakers baked an array of sweet breads, such as basil sour dough, raisin pudding and apple nut. Raisin pudding bread is my favorite. Leafy leeks and dark beets, mashed ruta-bagas and candied carrots were added. Sweet potatoes were topped with creamed goat's milk and hand shucked butter beans.

Yes, it was Thanksgiving, a time of festival and great celebration. Everyone gathered together for the yearly feast and awaited the weigh-in of Mr. Stickel's giant zuc-chini. It was a time of gratefulness, but not all are grateful at any time of year. Some people desire to be miserable, with stinky attitudes trying to take the joy out of every situation. They couldn't forget how the people they loved were starving and sick of being used and manipulated.

There is a Heavenly King. He is above all earthly kings and rules over the earth. His name is King Nissi. He must never be compared to a mere man. He is not mortal but immortal. Therefore, there is no comparison. He is above all human beings. The people prayed day and night to King Nissi, asking Him to release them from this evil king. He heard them as they prayed, but many years passed; and those who prayed in faith became discouraged, doubting the very existence of the King and some even dared to challenge His saving capabilities. He was not like the earthly king. He gave the people a gift—His very own Spirit who would reside with them and guide them into all truth and direction.

It was a full moon as I lay in my bed and beheld a bright light outside of my window. I leaped out of bed and tried not to wake my sister. My foot accidentally hit her in the head. Luckily, she's a sound sleeper, so she didn't move. I watched as condensation formed on the window from my very own breath. I had to wipe it away with the sleeve of my pajamas to see. The stars were bright in the sky, shining in such brilliance I had never seen before. I had never seen such an open sky.

I overheard my father and mum speaking in the living room. "Don't go, Reilly. Stay here with the kids and me." "I must go. I am a workman of the king." "Then, if you must go, be careful. I love you."

I heard the front door slam shut, and I accidentally knocked over the candle. Wax splattered on the walls and floor. "Yipson, get back to bed!" Mum yelled. I dove under my covers. How did Mum always know when I was out of bed? She wasn't even in my room. I overheard them talking, and I knew something was wrong. I didn't want anything to happen to him. I could hear the fear in Mum's voice.

A crowd of men surrounded the fields holding torches. Willfully, Father left our home and traveled to the castle by foot. I followed behind him, keeping a safe distance so no one would notice me. I hid in several bushes and trees. Several strong men tried to stop the guards from following Father.

Once at the castle, Father approached the king. The king began to throw slanderous accusations at him. It became unusually still and lightning flashed. The sky split apart and the earth below shook like an earthquake. An angel descended from the sky with a silver sword in his right hand. The angel was over seven feet in height with broad shoulders and long, flowing golden hair. He wore shiny metal armor and had the most piercing blue eyes. Fire came from his mouth and flowed down his long wintery hair. It did not burn his flesh and was everywhere.

The village trembled in fear, for an angel of destruction came swiftly near. He summoned King Ballot by name, his voice thundering as he spoke. "Your soul is completely vile, and you have no desire to change. Your mouth is corrupt, and the Heavenly King Nissi has had enough of your vileness! Do you think those who are wicked will continue to prosper in this way? Will the wrath of King Nissi come upon those who manipulate and hurt His people? Will He not repay? Let it be written that from this day forward a curse will be upon your reign, for you have defiled those who are innocent in pain. Their prayers have been heard, and their lives are not in vain."

"The kingdom you built for selfish ambition will be surrounded by rotted moss, and the stench will cause you to be sick to your stomach. And now you will suffer loss, for you have hurt those who worked tirelessly for you and did not care. You caused little children to cry and fall into deep despair. From this day forward when you receive food, it will rot before it touches your lips and you will brood in filth and despair. You will even lose the locks of your ratty hair. You will wish for death, but it will not come."

The king pleaded, "Please, please, the summoned host of King Nissi, will you not have mercy on me? I didn't mean to be cruel. I shouldn't have worked them in this way; I shouldn't have abused my rule. The angel had no sympathy for King Ballot; he was evil and his heart was undeserving.

The Spirit of King Nissi came over the angel like a thick, weighted cloud. Darkness hovered and immediately the angel had compassion on him. Lightning crackled in the sky; a piercing cry came from a bird flying by.

The angel held his breath. Then in a mighty wind, he exclaimed, "Very well, then, I will give you one hope.

There will only be one to break this curse upon your head, and the locks of her hair are red. Remember well everything I have spoken, for it cannot be reversed and will not be delayed." The angel receded into the earth, and the king was left to his cursed life.

As the years passed, the king grew more selfish, greedy and murderous. He sent his guards to search the village for a little girl with red hair. Mum feared the king would kill Caycee if he had the chance. She was not going to lose her daughter like other parents had in the past. She protected her to keep her safe. The king searched frantically for the girl who would remove the curse. Mum sewed Caycee a slouch hat to hide her red locks. She didn't want to lose her.

The king became weary from not eating. His tables were once filled with glutinous feasts. Now his face turned away from food, and the lack of nutrition robbed his bones. He ached. His chest sunk in and resembled a metal bird cage. The prophecy spoken over him continued, and although he wanted to die, death would not come to him.

Father knew if we lingered here any longer something bad would come about. He feared the king would begin to kill the people. He was not willing to take that chance with his own family! He gathered a small food supply, and Mum hurried us into the woods. Even though I was a wee boy, I remember the wind that night and the sound of leaves as we ran across them. I was afraid the guards might hear the sounds.

Wrapped in Caycee's arm was a fluffy brown teddy bear which she held tightly. A few men helped Father hoist the boat into the sea. They were strong men, and it took four of them working together. My father wanted them to go with us. I remember him asking them. They refused. They did not want to leave. They didn't like the king or queen, but they were comfortable where they were at.

Our father was not happy nor did he wish to stay under their rule any longer. He worked on an escape, and now the time was before us. We sailed in the dark for hours, and it was soothing to see the lights twinkle in the night sky. We were on an adventure. As my father steered the vessel, I heard him whistling the song he used to sing to Caycee and me every night before bed. The smell of freedom was in the air as our mum cried while holding us tightly. Our voices echoed in the night sky, but this time it was different. We were free, and we had no more limitations. *"One day when the winds are blowin' and the moon's light is showin', we'll be knowin', freedom is ours. We'll be lights on the ocean, free from commotion and we'll hold tight to each other knowin', freedom is ours."*

*"Freedom comes at a high cost;*
*it takes courage and strength.*
*To the one who fights with conviction and honor,*
*true victory awaits."*
(Nobel Reszen)

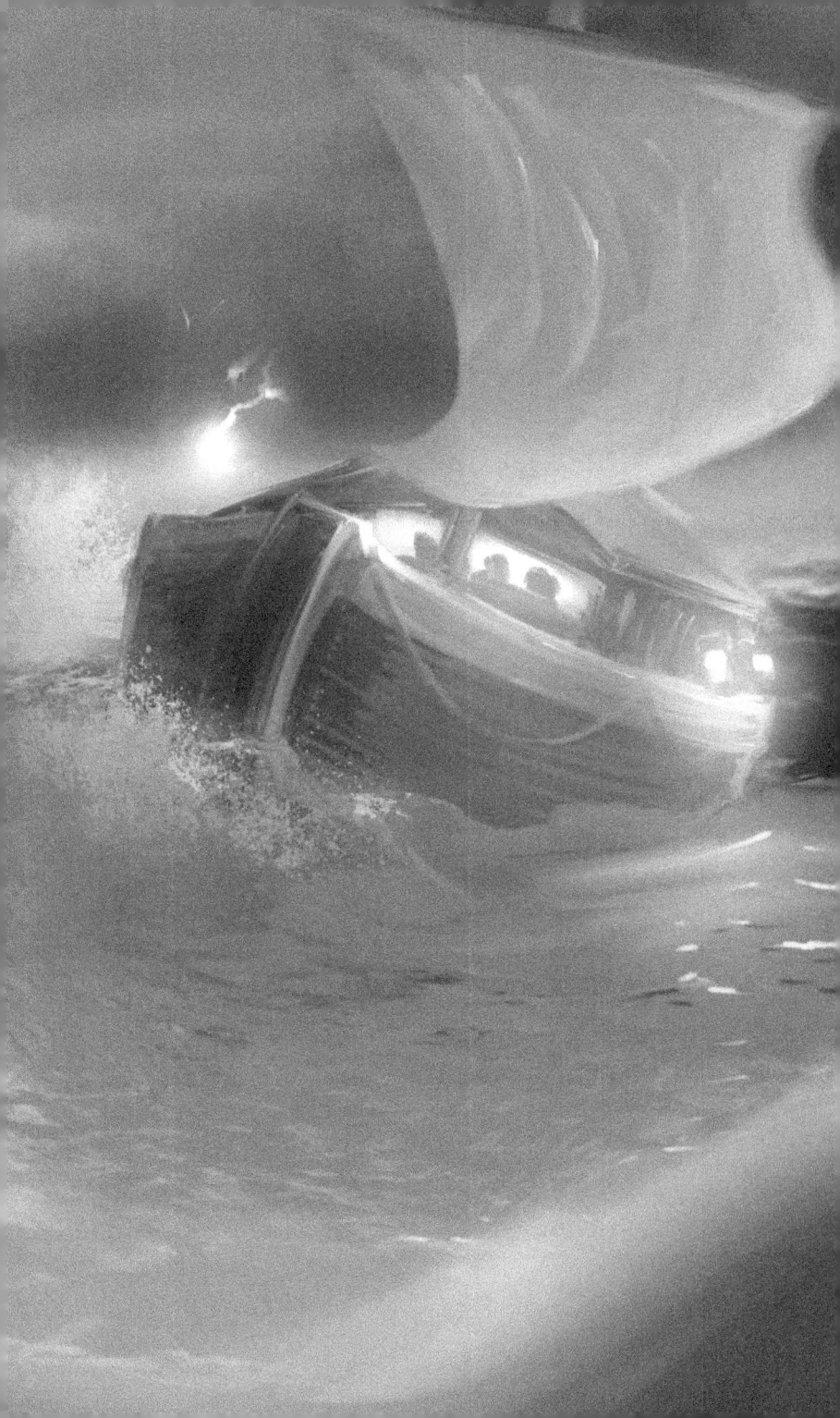

CHAPTER 5

# A Fierce Storm

# A Fierce Storm

ather set a course for us to the Wetlands, a place
located in the northern part of the world. The ocean
is no place for the weak of heart. One moment the
sun shines and birds dive down into the waters to capture
fish, and in an instant dark clouds moved in covering the
sun's light. The sky colors change from blue to gray like
in the snap of a finger. Lightning crackled and the sound
of thunder pierced the sky. We were sailing on my father's
ship, a sea worthy vessel with various almond colored
masks about.

A fierce storm was upon us that night. Intense rain
poured heavily, beating us down and leaving our bones
chilled. We were tired from fighting the rain all night.
The ship tossed back and forth violently as the sea began
to rise. We were in danger, because if the water rose, then
the ship would be swallowed by the ocean. Fearfully, I
watched as white caps crashed into the sides plopping
enormous amounts of water onto the decking. Within
minutes the lanterns lost their light, and we were in total
darkness. Oh, I shiver just remembering it!

I was terrified, but my sister Caycee maintained her courage. She gripped onto the rail of the ship with all her strength, holding on for dear life. With confidence she said, "It's going to be okay, everyone! We have made it this far, and nothing will stop us now."

Mum and Father fought tirelessly with the sails to keep us on the right pathway and keep the vessel from leaning too far over on either side. My heart pumped fast as my hands shook. I was sure I was having an anxiety attack. I suffer from those from time to time. The only way I ever found relief was when I asked King Nissi to help me. Now, I felt one coming on. Immediately I closed my eyes and began to pray quietly to myself. "King Nissi," I whispered. "If we make it out of this storm alive, then You are who I hear You are. One more request: Will You heal me from my panic attacks? They scare me. Okay, that is all!"

Suddenly the sky opened wide before us, the rain withdrew and the water receded. The sun's light radiated on my face and instantly warmed my weary body. I thought I was praying quietly, but Caycee must have heard me praying. She said, "It looks like King Nissi hears our prayers." "Yes," I agreed, and from that time on I was completely healed from the panic attacks. No more sweating, crazy heartbeats and feelings of panic or worry. Now, I did ask Him to make me taller, and I am still waiting for Him to answer. I have learned it's up to the King and what He decides.

We had been in darkness so long it took a minute for my eyes to adjust, but when they did, I noticed an island in front of us. My mind had often played tricks on me while traveling the ocean. Just to make sure I was not dreaming, I rubbed my eyes. "Father, look. I see land!" He took out his magnifying lens to confirm. What a sight to behold! It was magnificent! We were extremely happy! The waters had quieted down, and the landscape was serene. Pristine beaches, lush green grasses, mountains as high as the eye could see. Rolling fields of wildflowers brilliantly arrayed in every color of the rainbow.

Father reviewed his map and gauged our distance to the shore, for the storm had tossed us far from our original route and now we were further north. Looking at his map, he said, "This is an island, Evolone Hills. We are in the middle of nowhere!" "Isn't it grand?" Mum exclaimed. "Oh, Mum, I think it's just wonderful! Can we live here, please, please?"

Caycee grabbed Father's hat. She wanted to be in charge. She pretended to be a sea captain. "I could sing from the hills and dance in the tall grasses. I could even paint the ocean, pick rocks, climb hills, find treasures, make friends and there is so much more," said Caycee. "Yes, I am sure you could do all those things. Nothing is out of your reach, dear one," lovingly, he said.

We sailed into the bay of Evolone Hills watching the rocks beneath us. Father tied down the boat, and it felt nice to be on land. We met a few families who had settled on the island most recently. Possum jumped around and burping. Patsy Rose was just a pup, and she sniffed the ground like an ant eater. The people who lived in Evolone Hills were kindhearted and generous. They cared for each other, and they worked hard for their families.

It was a perfect place for our family to finally be free. It took a while for us to get used to it. They told tales of epic proportions. The monsters they spoke about were never small, but ginormous in size, having lizard-like skins and slimy tentacles like snakes circling the murky deep. Legend says these water beasts immersed from the deepest, darkest holes in the earth in search of their prey. No sea worthy vessel was ever safe from these ravenous hunters. Sleepless, they swam relentlessly through the waters seeking souls, charging ships and ramming their dragon-like bodies into their wooden sides, causing them to plummet into their dark watery graves.

*"The colors deep within the ocean are sapphire blue;*
*only a king can walk among them,*
*and each step you take He foreknew!"*
(Nobel Reszen)

CHAPTER 6

# Mrs. Glass

# Mrs. Glass

There were many families who settled on the island. They built homes and ran different businesses. The people who lived in Evolone Hills were known for their kindheartedness and generosity. They attended church and shared food with those who were needy. One and all cared for each other, and that is how is should be. Nevertheless, there are some strange ones who live here, which is not uncommon. Peculiar people like to hide in places of grandeur.

Father built a small shop in the village where he provided services for those who needed it. Woodworking was his passion, but being a blacksmith was his trade. He forged metals and fashioned them into hand tools or weapons. He also assisted with horseshoes. I paid close attention to how my father ran the family business. It was customary that one day I would be in charge. I was just beginning to learn the trade and was very intrigued at his work ethic and the process. He feared nothing and was willing to take on any project. He was dependable and dedicated. Often, he would let me take short breaks.

I could tell he was frustrated with me as I was learning, but he was still patient. He let me be a kid and enjoy life while I could.

For lunch, I would stroll down to Mrs. Glass. She had a book shop down the street. We called her Mrs. Glass because she made her store completely out of glass beads. It was quite a project, but she was an artist, creative and it suited her. The only way in the store was through a slide. I climbed the stairs and slid down the slide into a tub of colored cotton balls in colors of orange, red, green and blue. There was Mrs. Glass. "God be with you," she mumbled. I sat up and dusted the cotton balls off my leggings.

"So, what can I do you for, Yipson?" I, of course, noticed a dusty old unorganized space behind the shop. I pointed and said, "I think I'll check out what you have over there!" "Go right ahead," she said without hesitation. "You never know, you may find a few jumping spiders among hidden things." "I am a boy and spiders don't bother me," I said as I bit my fingernails.

I hate spiders. They send shivers up my spine. Every now and then I am confronted with a nasty spider scurrying about my home. Spiders don't fool me a bit, even though they pretend to be dead, I know their folly, those creepy crawly fakers.

In a dark corner I noticed a dusty, pitiful looking book, completely left to rot. How hideous of someone to hate such a wonderful literary work. Curious, I picked it up, dusted it off and it appeared familiar to me. I sneezed several times from the dust bunnies which climbed into my nostrils, and then a nasty spider jumped on my arm. I screamed and then the spider rolled over on its side faking its own death. I took the book and hit the spider on its head. I heard a faint laugh and then silence.

I quickly rolled over to Mrs. Glass to check out the book. She didn't seem to be bothered at all! "Take it for all I care. No one has looked at that book for years." She turned away from me, but a mirror on the wall revealed a smirk she was trying to hide. I lugged the book over my shoulder. "It's heavy!" I whined. "I'll help you out." Mrs. Glass pushed me up the slide. I maneuvered my way down the stairs carefully so I wouldn't drop my book.

This dictionary I held in my hands was written by a renowned professor named Nobel Reszen, born in 1777. He was what was known as a **"ramplewhinnelmelon"** meaning *extremely odd and old man*. He grew up on the island way before any settlers lived there. He was one of the founding fathers, you could say. Professor Nobel Reszen was one of the original settlers to Evolone Hills. People tend to gossip about others, and many embellished stories were spoken throughout the generations regarding his odd and peculiar behavior.

People think writers are often a bit unusual and eccentric. They are curious about their imaginations and their abilities. I think they are supernatural. Something happens in the mind of a writer, for they see the world not as some do, but in their eyes different, vibrant and filled with imagination. Not everyone understands this. As Professor Nobel so eloquently says, "They are "**Blastednappers**" meaning *stealers of joy and happy literary thoughts.*

"*Blastednappers tend to steal creativity in writers because of their covetous heart and jealous manners*" (Nobel Reszen). There were many stories about his life and legacy floating around the people. They believed he was insane. He was known for his extremely odd behavior. For instance, he caused a "**Lortwallscene**" meaning *running and tickling oneself with an uncanny excitement.* It was not uncommon for him to parade throughout the village expressing odd behaviors. For Instance, one morning he was standing on the rooftop of the village floral shop, bobbing his head in and out of rain clouds. "**Pufferheadmaddle**" meaning *a person who likes his head in clouds.*

Secondly, he owned seventeen tiger-striped cats named "BobbyBugglebees." Oddly enough, their names were all the same.

Thirdly, Nobel became an author at the age of seven. Most children at his age were fascinated with catching wriggly frogs and capturing slimy sea turtles by the ocean, but certainly not Nobel. He was burrowed in the sand near a rock writing a novel using a sap pen made from **whippalysapwood** meaning *a specialty wood which is not porous and can hold liquid ink.* He wrote seventy-seven literary marvels about his feline companions, the BobbyBugglebees. However, he compiled a legendary dictionary of Irish words, and you have already read some excerpts throughout the pages of my writings.

Inside the pages of Nobel's dictionary are the definitions from his legendary works. I am using them in this story with copyright permission, of course. I officially hold in my hands the only copy of his masterpiece, and there is no other per da'commins alive that I am aware of. I was brave enough to talk to the professor most ignored about his advances, and they don't have his dictionary now, do they? He was a true per **da'commins** meaning *a true literary genius.*

Nobel chose solitude most of the time to ponder and write. One must have some time to reflect and concentrate on the task at hand.

One dreary afternoon, I decided to take an unexpected trip into town. Mum asked me to grab her some apples. Professor Nobel stood discreetly in front of me. I noticed something rather unsettling coming from his bottom—a black tail protruded, swaying back and forth. I was **"prolump'la'groops"** meaning *a state of unbridled confusion, confused.* He spun around with great excitement grinning. Quite chipper, he whispered, "Boy, always remember that BobbyBugglebees are affectionate creatures who admire their masters and listen attentively to their commands. Did you know when you tickle their bellies, they can laugh on demand?"

One day I overheard a village officer rallying the people of the village. He was calling a tent meeting to discuss the usage of the village water. Everyone was encouraged to meet down by the shore. Nobel attended the meeting, and sat quickly in the back while a crowd of people gathered in front of him. I tried not to stare at him as he was dressed in strange linens. I never saw a man before who wore turquoise sashes.

I couldn't help myself, and out of my peripheral vision I saw him raise his hand and motion for me to come closer. I was intrigued by his odd nature. Curiousness burned within me. What on earth could he want with me? I got up from my chair and walked towards him. He handed me a dictionary. Bound in leather, he told me, "This will be of excellent value someday."

He disappeared and I heard a hissing sound and noticed a shadow of a cat creeping across the pole holding up the tent. I believe that he was not just a man, but a mancatal. My father told Caycee and me a story about him before. Yes, that is right, and don't judge me! I believe Professor Nobel is half cat and half human! Sure, logically it does not make much sense, but you must remember that this is an Irish tale. **Mancatal** meaning *a feline and a human, a whimsical fantasy furman.*

Unfortunately, I never could prove my suspicion that Nobel was of mancatal status because he died at the age of seventy-seven. His body was never found, and he had no service or funeral. Legend says he swam out to sea and never returned. He must have drowned or a ship picked him up and he relocated away from the island. He never married nor had any children of his own.

Rumspun rumors surfaced all over the village, and the people gossiped about what happened to him. **Rumspun** meaning *false accusations*.

Legend says he was killed by a pack of wild creatures who roamed about named **Da'Ha'Lilies** meaning *fairy-like creatures with purple noses studded with rings, nasty sharp teeth and fluffy marshmallow jagged wings*. They only came when high winds covered the hills. Others supposed a fish in the ocean swallowed him whole, then spit his bones out and they sunk to the bottom of the ocean.

On a windy day sea captains claim you could hear Professor Nobel's bones chatter, sounding like a wind chime. Others assume he must have died of a broken and lonely heart and suffered a **"moparoo"** meaning *a sad estate of pitiful sorrow*. Truthfully, no one really knows what happened at the time of his death.

Before he died, he planted seven trees along seven winding paths which led to his home. Each tree intertwines, creating a pathway of enchantment. Bobby-bugglebums are long-haired, furry black cats with green glowing eyes and black wings. Each of them has a rope around their neck with a golden coin. When the moon is full, their howls can be heard throughout the valley. They perch themselves on a twisted tree, resting their claws on the branches for stability. The bobbybuggle-bums wallow in utter agony like a pack of wild wolves longing to share their hunt with one another. Their eyes glow 'til the morning light.

*"Cats are divine and canny in nature,*
*but bobbybugglebums are true feline innovators,*
*not intimidators."*
(Nobel Reszen)

CHAPTER 7

# The Open Gate

# The Open Gate

In the midnight hour, suddenly I awoke from gently swaying in my bed. Flooding the night sky was the eerie cries of bobbybugglebums. I could hardly keep my eyes open, but that didn't stop me from traveling down the dreary path. The wind beat against the trees and I dreaded the Da'Ha'Lilies. It was possible they could fly in at any moment.

When I arrived at the gate, the wind abruptly stopped. It was spookily quiet, and the gate began to swing all by itself. Should I turn around and go back? Oh, the life of an Irish man! "Suppose this place is haunted," I thought to myself. The beams of the moon were like a spotlight. It took my eyes a moment to adjust.

Mysteriously, seven roads appeared. Which way should I go? Where do they lead? I was confused and unsure about which road to choose. I should have turned around and went back home, but I couldn't. The calls of the bobbybugglebums beckoned me. I began to walk down the center road. I chose the straight and narrow pathway. With each step I took, a tree appeared and in the branches was the green glow of their piercing eyes. I was being watched, and I heard the ruffling of their wings.

One flew down to the lower branch and began to speak to me. "Yipson, you have been chosen. Never let the treasure go." He explained to me that they are the watchers of the book that Professor Nobel gave to me. They are the witnesses to the literary works of his hands.

I felt a presence beside me, and it was not a bobby-bugglebum. I turned around and only saw a shadow. To this day, I still believe it was the Professor. I thanked him for the watchers, and I needed to get home. They bid me farewell and said in parting, "We will always be near. When you call on us, we will hear."

I don't like to get caught up in superstitious beliefs, although I am quite aware there is another world around me—an active spiritual world filled with various dimensions that truly need to be explored. My father spoke of it often in his stories and nighttime tales. He alleged that he saw creatures which could not be explained. They were bright in colors and filled with light—supernatural light.

I think the professor was such a person—supernatural and set apart. Sadly, there was no living relatives to claim his staggering wealth. His literary agent made out well, sending himself royalty checks and used his copyright to reproduce a book about laughing cats, the bobbybugglebum laugh in trees. It was a number one seller on the island and brought him great revenue.

The agent was aware of one literary marvel he had yet to capitalize from: the dictionary of the professor. He used his seducing charm to try and gain the treasure from the beloved Mrs. Glass, known for her unique collections of oddities, rare records and paperback magazines. He pretended to like her, but she was wise and didn't fall for his advances.

Poor Professor Nobel, he probably should have read the fine print below his signature on the contract he signed with his agent. Even the most talented, educated people can make blunders and fall into a **"Cave of notions"** meaning *a secretive agenda filled with toxic potion.* All of us learn lessons in life; some are harder to swallow than others.

*"The world is filled with people who*
*merely perceive a matter but never truly*
*understand a matter."*
(Nobel Reszen)

CHAPTER 8

# An Irish Tale

# An Irish Tale

Caycee and I treasured exploring the Hills. We were on an adventure and seeking treasures. Of course, she was faster than me because she had longer legs, but I didn't let that stop me. I rolled alongside her quite fine. I was known as being "the instigator." To say, "I like to poke a little too much" would be an understatement. At one time or another I believe all of us are guilty of stirring the pot. We push buttons of those who are close to us.

I enjoyed poking my sister in the side of her leg, thus agitating her and eventually provoking her to anger. Her response generally was to smack me on the top of my head in love. You know, I think everything sounds better with love attached to it. How about, "I am going to let you have it in love"?

Caycee would simply ignore my intentional, often infuriating advances. She kept a good outlook on life and situations, so her creativity would never fail her. She enjoyed gazing at the clouds in the sky and watching them take shape. She could see anything with her imagination.

I was inspired by her will to look at the bright side of things. No matter what we faced, she kept a great perspective and always managed to smile. I always said, "I could be serious for the both of us." Why so serious? I don't know. It's what those who are responsible do. We tend to be overly concerned with much and easily lose sight of the important things.

After sailing on the ship for years, it is comforting to us to be gently rocked to sleep. It was not like every child's room, for our father built our beds with wood platforms. He used chains and secured them to the wooden beams on the ceiling. We could rock all night if we wished. We were nestled in our floating beds, waiting to hear the footsteps of our father. It was pure excitement when we heard him coming. The floorboards creaked as he entered the room. "It appears my wee children are ready for a bedtime fable."

He placed a hot cup of tea on the bedside table and held a wax candle close to him. We watched the shadows the candlelight cast on the wall. "Deep in the ocean, far from the shores of men, a mother whale, pregnant, wrestles to give birth from a dark hole much like a fox den. Sea creatures gather around watching, waiting with great anticipation. The creatures who watched needed some hot tea."

"Awe. Father," Caycee said. "Let me take a sip of my tea." Both of us waited patiently in anticipation. We knew that if we didn't, Father would not finish the story. "Okay, where was I? Ah, yes. After the mother whale pushed and

pushed, a head popped out. A golden whale? No, this was no ordinary whale. It was a dragon-like creature with wings.

"Everyone watched with anticipation. It certainly did not look like a mere whale. What was it? Where did it come from? All the sea creatures watching knew this was no ordinary sea pup. This whale had a unicorn horn on his head. All the sea creatures glared at the pup in amazement. Suddenly his mother became protective of her child and scared them away by thrashing her body to and fro."

My sister enjoyed listening and watching her father's facial expressions while telling us the story. He was quite amusing to her. I, of course, needed some attention and began to poke Caycee in the leg. Father looked down at his cup of tea, and I took my opportunity thinking he could not see my sneakiness. I forgot one thing. He has great peripheral vision. Fathers are never oblivious to naughty behavior when it comes to their children. Never forget! Adults were once young too. Even though depending on his mood, he would let me get away with it. I still knew the look when I was busted! "Yipson, stop aggravating your sister." "Yes, Father," I replied. I turned my head in sorrow for an added effect of drama, meanwhile sticking my tongue out to my sister behind my father's back. Caycee's eyes became heavy. She was exhausted. After all, I spent most of my waking hours aggravating her.

Father continued. "The ocean was dark. The newborn creature rested next to his mother with his eyes gently closed. Night had fallen swiftly, and the moon could faintly be seen. There was a squawk in the midnight sky. Something began to slide down the moon's beam! The baby whale's horn began to glow like a star, like diamonds shimmering in the ocean."

"All right, that is it for now. The both of you, it's time for bed!" "Father, no! You must finish the story; you simply must," Caycee exclaimed. "Children, it is time for bed," Mum yelled. Father kissed us good-night, and we fell fast asleep.

I remember my mother watching us rest. I pretended to be asleep. I peeked at her with one eye, and she laughed and covered me up with a blanket. Mum treasured laughter, for she possessed a cheerful heart. No matter what happened in life, she would find the noblest perspective bestowing her faith as a good example to all.

There is a lot to gain from a person with such wisdom and reverence for her children. My mum understood that life was not in her hands, but in greater and more powerful ones, the hands of King Nissi.

"An Irish tale enchants the soul."
(Nobel Reszen)

CHAPTER 9

# The Deep Woods

# The Deep Woods

Inside the house was cozy. The fire was crackling and bubbly beef stew was steaming in a black cast iron pot. I was to be doing my chores, but I didn't feel like doing a blasted thing. I wanted to have a lazy day, full of daydreams and snacks. Whatever mood possessed me, I felt as though Professor Nobel had a perfect word just for my current predicament. It was **"hoozyazydays"** meaning *days where you would rather snooze than do any or all manual labor (no chores or responsibilities)*. That is me! I am having a hoozyazyday! Can I get a **"whoppen-toe"**? This means *a credible witness with extended arms.*

The woods certainly were no place to be in the late fall. Many dangerous animals lived in the woods, especially mean, scary wolves. They were famished and liable to eat anything or anyone who crossed their paths. They were vicious with snarly, yellowish teeth and piercing eyes. You would think maybe I would be cautious of the furry beasts. I ran through the thick brush singing, skipping and certainly not paying any attention to the forest ground beneath me. **"Curpaplunked"** meaning *when an* *individual unexpectedly falls to the ground.* I unexpectedly fell to the ground, and my face was covered with mud. I wiped the debris from my eyes and laid on the ground contemplating, "Did anyone see me?" Of course, this was a crazy thought since I am in the middle of nowhere!

It took a few minutes to compose myself while mustering the strength to get upright again. I eventfully managed to get up. I noticed an out of place branch oddly wiggling behind a tree not very far from me. Curiously I thought, "What could it be?" Then I heard a low menacing growl accompanied with heavy breathing. Instantly, I began to panic. Surely I was not alone in these woods. Stuttering, I exclaimed "Oh, no, the grey wolves!"

Have you ever been so scared out of your mind that you don't even know what to say? That is exactly what happened to me. Every hair on my neck and back stood upright. At the very moment, I had deep regret because I disobeyed my mum. I wished I had listened and did my chores like a good, obedient son should. If only I would have listened, I would not be out here, ready to be eaten alive by a horrible beast. Worst of all, I have short legs. How will I outrun him? It was then that the wolf squatted down and snarled yellow teeth near my face.

My short life flashed before my eyes. I was too young to die. I wanted to live! "Let me live," I shouted! To my amazement, a rock catapulted, hitting the grey wolf. Delivering a crashing blow to the side of his head, he fell over, knocked out, completely unconscious. I thought to myself, "What just happened? Where did that rock come from?" Then I heard a voice, "Are you okay?" Well, I'll be a stuffed guzzler in a basketball hoop! It was my sister!

"Are you a sight to see!" I said to her. It is amazing what a life or death situation will do for your sibling relationship. Normally, I would rather poke her in the leg, but at this moment I wanted to give her the biggest bear hug ever! Caycee's slingshot skills have always been extraordinary. Father taught her well. She could hit anything with only one shot. She knocked a Noorwal out, and they have the hardest heads around. **Noorwals,** which means *a strange, hard-headed, six-horned aquatic deer with miniature fur-like fins and ears which can whistle.*

Caycee took a stick and poked the wolf in his side. The wolf did not move, but she noticed his chest slightly rising and he was still breathing. "We need to get out of here. The wolf is still breathing, shallow but still breathing." She said, "Wait till I tell Mum what you were up to, older brother. You will have some explaining to do."

"My dearest sister, you wouldn't!" "Well, let's see how fast you can run, my short brother. Whoever gets home first!" Caycee skipped off evilly laughing. Meanwhile, all I could think is how much trouble I was going to be in. "Why did I go into the thick woods alone? Why couldn't I just do my chores like a good lad? Why do I always get distracted?"

Caycee made it to the house first. but I was a close second behind her. I figured it was better to tell the truth than to lie. So I mustered up the courage and blurted out, "I went into the woods alone, and I know it was wrong.

I almost got attacked by a wolf, but I am okay. Caycee saved me, and now I am home again. Isn't that grand?"

No truer words could have been spoken. For it is always better to tell a **Frameba** than to tell a lie. **"Frameba"** means *a true statement*. There are times in our minds we wish to do the very opposite. We know what is the right thing to do, but often we choose to do the wrong thing. For some reason we think we won't have any consequences for our disobedience. You may get away with it now, but you won't always get away with things.

"Where have you been?" Mum asked rather perturbed. I hesitated to respond. Mum knew I was up to no good. You couldn't hide anything from her at all. She saw right through me to my very soul. Caycee sat back, cleverly smirking at my predicament. At least Possum cared and was trying to lick my face, and her breath always smelled like rotted fish and moldy pudding. Patsy Rose whimpered and in between the two, Mum was momentarily distracted. Slurp! Slurp! Not another lick! My face was completely covered by saliva from her slippery tongue.

Caycee did what she always does. She makes me laugh. She made the silliest face, crossing her eyes, protruding her jaw. "Who do I remind you of?" she asked. Possum made the same facial expression as she looked over towards her. Simultaneously, both of us started laughing hysterically. Possum was not like a dog or a cat, but oddly strange. In the north land, her type of breed was called a **"Jackumm"** meaning *a combination of a possum, a kangaroo and a tree gopher slightly mixed together creating a fearless pet with wiry hair and strong dialect.* Their breed is known to be fun loving, calm and offers impeccable protection as a natural guard pet. I would like to mention, Jackumms are valued for their sense of humor, boundless recollection and cartoon-like teeth. There is one thing that is not so neat. They have extremely bad gas when falling into a deep sleep. They are not very good swimmers; they tend to float, but they are protective and extremely loyal. They may also have food aggression when eating their bunches of wheat. One must never interrupt them during their feeding time.

Father found Possum as he traveled to Humpfrim Island in search for boulder rocks and sea treasures. He found Possum alone and sickly. She was abandoned by her mother and left to die. He decided to rescue her and bring her home to the family. He wrapped her in a blanket and brought her home. When I first saw her, I was curious. I knew she was not a dog and certainly not a cat. Either way I figured I could get used to that!

Caycee, on the other hand, loved her because she was unique. I noticed Possum favored Caycee over me. They say animals can sense things about humans, and I was an aggravator at times. Brothers tend to aggravate their sisters from time to time. Regardless of our shortcomings, we are a family and we will love each other in spite of our many differences.

*"Everyone has colors when you choose to see;
when celebrated joyfully they blend together splendidly."*
(Nobel Reszen)

CHAPTER 10

# An Expected Guest

# An Expected Guest

The island was a tourist hot spot, and when travelers visited they would pass through her establishment. Madam Mamsie owned a bed and breakfast in the village. It wasn't a large place, but rather quaint, not like a sprawling estate or anything, but cozy. She offered guest rooms with great nightly rates. Two bedrooms fully furnished were upstairs.

Mamsie used to teach drama, and she was great at arranging plays and skits. She was known for her creative dishes and made a mean **Wafflewingtwook**—*a large, fluffy waffle shaped like a winged angel with whimsical maple syrup drippings and powdered sugar topping.* Stocked on a shelf were a variety of fresh berry jams, apple pies, candied prunes, strawberry jelly, apricot scones, cherry dumplings, rhubarb bread, butterscotch fudge and peanut butter chocolate bars, each weighing one pound apiece.

Then, beyond the hallway was a spiral staircase leading to a loft area known as the pig suite. Sows of all colors and sizes hung on the walls. The staff who worked for her put on quite a show for the quests and visitors. It was like a dinner theater. There was no shortage of songs, and dancing was allowed, with an occasional singing mouse named Peter.

Singing mice are quite rare, but Professor Nobel wrote about them in his dictionary. "**Minnyboasters**" means *a tiny breed of mice who utilize their diaphragm to sing boastfully, engaging in beautifully composed theatrical melodies.* He had lived there for many years, wrapped in a tiny hole by the floorboard. Peter watched many people come and go. Food was easy for him to come by. He gathered the table scraps. Madam Mamsie let him reside in her place because he kept her wooden floors free of fallen food.

The rules were that he could not be seen by human eyes. Now, if he was performing a song or dancing a jig, that was a different story. She catered to all, but she had an attraction for certain men—men who were good-looking and extremely wealthy. She daydreamed that one day she would meet a dashing, handsome prince. He would be good-looking and have a full head of hair and, of course, he would be extremely wealthy. This dreamy prince would sweep her off her feet, marry her and they would live happier ever after, with a couple of children.

Madam Mamsie only had eyes for one such captain, Lord Gregory. He was tall, handsome, wealthy and had an extremely long beard with a distinct white line running down the middle of it. He was the "catch of the sea," as she put it so eloquently.

I admired many things about Madam Mamsie. I had never seen such dresses and elaborate colored fabrics as what she had. Lord Gregory spoiled her every year when he returned his ship to Evolone. My father had fashioned steel cages, which she used as petticoats underneath her dresses. The staff was fitted by a seamstress, and measurements were given to my father. He carefully followed the plans and created one-of-a-kind soldiered steel cages for each of them. They were heavy to lift, and so was Madam Mamsie. Lord Gregory didn't mind. He liked his women rather large in stature.

It was love at first sight. They stared into each other's eyes and hearts formed in each pupil. In fact, hearts formed all around them. It was as if they were floating on the clouds. Lord Gregory had a son named Dylan. Unfortunately, his mum died when he was born so he raised him by himself with the occasional help of a nanny! He was a widower. This worked out great for Mamsie. She had never been married.

Dylan was close with only a few people in the village. He took a liking to my sister. Instantly they became friends, best friends. I knew that Dylan liked Caycee, even though he would never admit it. I noticed the way he looked at her and the way he poked at her. Every time he was around her, his voice would deepen and his chest would protrude forward. Sometimes I wondered if he thought he was a wild turkey. They stick their chests out when they approach a female turkey. But I never saw any feathers on him, and believe me, I was looking!

I told you that strange people live here. I hope you haven't forgotten that Professor Nobel had a tail from his bottom. One must always be **"Keevertious"** meaning *mysterious and watchful of current illusions.*

Caycee and Dylan were inseparable, laughing, sharing stories and both loved to play pranks on me. One time they decided to puncture a hole in my water bucket. I just couldn't understand by the time I got home why my bucket was empty. They laughed at the trail I left behind. I never found that funny. They both had red curly hair, and Dylan is a little more on the wild side. His hair stuck up on all ends. I found it quite comical.

Possum didn't like Dylan, and he would randomly kick him from time to time. Dylan tried to jump on her back and ride her like a horse. That was **"Ripoaklopp"** meaning *stupid or dumb.* She didn't like that a bit. Dylan would curl his body up as if he were a soccer ball, and Possum gave him a good kick and knocked him clear across the field. Caycee and I laughed with delight when he flew past the hay bales and hay was stuck in his crazy hair. He never hurt himself; it's just that his ego was bruised.

*"True loyalty is found in divine royalty."*
(Nobel Reszen)

Chapter 11

# A Daydream

# A Daydream

Not a day went by when I didn't find myself day-dreaming of sailing on the mighty ocean with my family. Oh, I cherished the sea. Patsy Rose and I went for a stroll along the shore, and it wasn't long before I was resting on a rock and watching the clouds move across the sky. I fell into a deep sleep and before I knew it I was dreaming.

We were sailing and I was nestled into Possum's pouch for warmth. My father was holding my mum and Caycee right by her side, tugging on her skirt. Menacing clouds passed by and golf-size hail catapulted down from the heavens, violently shaking the waters. A rushing wind barreled towards the sailboat. It was cold and dark, and our hope grew faint. A large wave rushed to the sailboat. It crashed upon the boat and threw us overboard. Mum swam frantically trying to reach us. Caycee and I held each other tightly. The waves carried Caycee and me away from our parents, and we could no longer see them. Our eyes were burning from the salt water. We could barely keep them open.

Caycee kept burping from swallowing too much water. "Yipson, do you think we will be all right?" she cried. "I don't know, Caycee. I don't know."

The cries of Mum and Father were faint, and all we saw was the light of the moon. Then, I felt a rushing under my legs. It was Possum. We placed our feet in his pouch, filled with water It was warmed by his stomach. Possum swam through the waters like a seal.

I felt so safe in Possum's pouch I feel asleep. I was exhausted and fell into a deep sleep. Caycee laid her head on my chest, and I held her tightly. She whimpered, and I knew she missed Mum and Father. All we could do now was pray. We had lost all hope.

When morning came, Possum licked my hair trying to comfort me. She had the worst breath ever. I was tired, hungry and seasick. I began to hear the cries of my mum and father, and my vision became blurry. I saw my mum, and she had her arms stretched out toward me, but I couldn't get to her. She was wearing a white gown, and she looked young and rested.

"Yipson, you must live. Don't give up. Take care of your sister. She needs you," she said gently. Then I woke up! It was only a dream! Thank King Nissi, it was only a dream! I went home and gave my mom the biggest hug. I was thankful she was alive. I wish to never have that dream again!

# A Daydream

*"Dreams are rarely as they seem;*
*they have hidden meanings and some are oddly themed!"*
(Nobel Reszen)

CHAPTER 12

# Legend Says

# Legend Says

You would not believe the tales I have heard over the years. This one I remember quite vividly. Legend says that every thousand years or so a golden bird dragon descends where no light abides, and it is there where she will give birth to hundreds of eggs, but only one will possess a special power. Not just any power, but a supernatural power.

The egg will begin to swirl through the ocean beaming with rainbow lights. The waves will toss the egg gently until it forms a golden crackle throughout. The rays of light from the sun will bring tiny particles of shimmering light that look like gold over the egg. The golden egg will cover itself until the light of a full moon awakens it.

In the darkness part of the night, some say that it is a bewitching hour—a time when those who are evil have their way, but that is not true. It is quite the contrary. The moon reflects the light of the sun. The light is the dragon's sign to awaken from its slumber. The golden dragon is protected by guard fish called *Tee'ah-stone'whens who* magically appear to guard the precious egg. Tee'ahstone'whens are oversized sea otters with yellow heads, pudgy noses, reddish horns and burly brown tummies. They defend the egg with their very life refusing to let it out of their sight. They are great swimmers and have a distinct humming sound which they use to communicate with each other under water.

When the full moon appears in the midnight sky, the egg emerges from the dark swallows of the ocean and rests under the moon's light. The light penetrates the egg, and the shell breaks. A golden dragon rises by the moon's light, and follows the beams to a secret cave. It is there that the dragon closes his eyes and hibernates for many years.

Golden dragons cannot see natural light until they are fully grown. No human can ever see the dragon until it reaches maturity. Its wings must be formed, fire breathing techniques cultivated and the proper weight must be gained. Once mature, the dragon will not allow just anyone to enter his dwelling. It is said that the gold given to the dragon is from another world, a supernatural world. No death resides in this supernatural place—only peace and tranquility. No sickness, no war and no death, only life. It is a heavenly place where no darkness is allowed.

The river which flows there is pure and undefiled by human hands. A light is so pure that understanding flows from its beams and dances inside of each soul who lives there. To enter, one must possess a childlike faith and humility. No pride can be in one's heart to enter. They must be pure in word and in deed.

*"There are mysteries hidden in the deep blue sea;
tales hold the keys to see unfathomable things."*
(Nobel Reszen)

CHAPTER 13

# The Secret Cave

# The Secret Cave

One fall afternoon, Caycee, Patsy Rose and I combed through the seashells and stones on the shore. We found treasures, broken pieces of glass and colored rocks. The tide was dangerous, but we took our chances. Adventure knows no boundaries. On the east side of the island is where we were, and bountiful green pine trees and stone mountains surrounded us.

One place was off limits. It was told as a legend that a great lesson was learned here. An ancient stone archway was built thousands of years ago, before Evolone Hills was ever inhabited by people. A sign was carved above it in old Celtic scrabbling which read, "No one can enter this place, except one of bravery and grace." I was leery because Caycee was getting very close to the archway.

Patsy Rose darted into the water, and I went after her. I saw Caycee bend down and pick up two shiny stones, and then she disappeared for a moment. I heard her voice, but I couldn't see her. "Yipson, come look. I found gold!"

"Where in great murffin are you?" I asked. "Over here," she said in a muffled voice. Then she appeared. In disbelief, I ventured over to her, and to my surprise it was gold, real gold. I was dumbfounded! "Where did you find these?"

"Over there," she pointed her finger to the stone archway. Immediately I knew what she had done. "You went beyond the archway?" "Yes, I did." "You are never to do that! What is wrong with you! You know the stories, the legend told of the stone archway. You are never to go there, especially by yourself."

"Oh, stop being a parent, Yipson. Sometimes you are just too safe!" Legend says men and women alike crossed the archway and never returned to Evolone Hills.

"Look, Yipson, I'll just stick my foot under it."

I cringed as Caycee extended her right leg under the archway. It disappeared right before our eyes. Something else happened. The temperature drastically changed. Light snowflakes fell and goosebumps spread up and down my arms. It felt as though it was winter. I desperately wanted to stop her from going any further, but a force stronger than me stopped me dead in my tracks. It was as if my flesh was fearful, but in my soul I was at peace. The archway turned twice and the ground became white with snow. The wind howled and blew violently.

Caycee disappeared. "Hello, Hello, is anyone in here?" she yelled. Her voice echoed. The legend of the cave was passed down from generation to generation. A fierce fire-breathing dragon lived in there, and no human could ever enter or they would be burned alive if they considered his eyes and if they saw his whole body. They would turn into a pillar of pure gold.

Two green eyes, piercing and glowing, appeared before her. They swayed back and forth and blinked and glared at her intently. Caycee trembled. She was shivering from the wintry weather.

"Show yourself, dragon!" Her hair flew back and her cheeks fluttered as the dragon was sniffing her, and then he sneezed right in her face. "Yuk," she exclaimed. "What are you doing here?" the dragon shouted. "You shouldn't be here," shaking his head.

"I have every right to be here. This is my land. This is where I live," Caycee replied. "Is it true that you can spit fire?" she asked the dragon in disbelief. The dragon replied, "Yes, I can breathe fire, spit fire and throw fire."

"Then why are we in the dark?" she asked. She desired to see the fire-breathing dragon, plus she was cold and hoped the light would warm her up. He breathed on the wall, and four candles appeared. The dragon stepped back from the light.

"Can I see you?" she requested. "What if you are afraid?" "I shall not be afraid." The dragon took his tail and knocked over a couple of rocks from a rock wall until it came right in front of Caycee. "Sit down on my tail. Go on now!"

Caycee leaped onto his tail, boasting a curious grin. A beam of light came flooding in the cave. It was not enough light to see his full body, only a silhouette of his body. From his silhouette, she could see he was very large—over 20 feet high and very wide. He had large wings on his sides, a very long tail and two horns protruding from his egg-shaped head.

"I think you are magnificent!" The dragon used his tail to knock a few more rocks down from the pile, and it provided just enough light for her to see him fully now. Caycee was in amazement. It was a spectacular sight. She had never seen a dragon before. The dragon was brilliant, shimmering gold in color and covered with luminous scales. His wings were the colors of the rainbow, and they were reflective in the dark. He sparkled like a diamond with flecks of gold throughout his reptile-looking skin.

He had broad shoulders and a strong neck, beefy legs and massive claws, which resembled crescent moons, four on each foot. The color of his eyes was florescent lime-green pupils, largely round with elongated lashes. His nose, though prominent, was small for his size; and he had cat whiskers on both sides of his mouth and a tail like a slithering snake.

"Come into the light, dragon," she said fearlessly. Frolick leaned into the light and Caycee looked like a jelly bean compared to the gold dragon. "What shall I call you?"

"My name is Sir Frolick," he replied. "You're not scary at all." Caycee looked at all the pictures of the dragon on the cave walls. "Why are all these pictures carved into the rocks?"

I have lived here for centuries and these are my writings, the story of my life here in the cave. Caycee pointed to one towards the back of the cave. "I especially like the one where you are eating berries, Is that a double chin?" Sir Frolick was self-conscience of it.

"Do you think I am large?" He felt insecure about his weight gain over the years. "Not at all, I think you are rather funny and cute. I love your chins," laughing. Sir Frolick gently dropped her from his tail and vanished for just a moment, and then returned with a red shirt on. Obviously, it was too small for him; it had shrunk. He sat on a rock and crossed his legs. Then his face changed, his nostril flared and his tail straightened.

They were not alone in the enchanted cave. Dragons don't like unexpected visitors "Who do we have here?" Sir Frolick asked as his tiny feet dangled to and fro.

"Wait one minute." Caycee removed my cloak. "Yipson, how did you get in here?" she asked. I didn't want her to be in the cave alone. After all, he was her big brother. I thought big brothers are to protect their little sisters. Sir Frolick sniffed my head, "You smell like old onions, and I like old onions," he said in a surly voice. Sir Frolick literally scared the wool socks right off me! Seriously, when he smelled my head. I thought he was going to eat me. Plus, he loved onions and I smelled like one.

I was in a **lumpersoomopple** meaning *a horrible circumstance, a pickle of a predicament.* "Why did I slurp a bowl of onion soup for lunch? I love onion soup!" she said. "You do? I couldn't let you go alone. I have been listening, and I have been here all along," he replied.

Caycee begged Sir Frolick to put me down. I should have known better. Curiousness got the better of me. After all, I was Caycee's big brother; and when we were not at the house I was to be watching her. It was my responsibility.

Sir Frolick and Caycee played and laughed, talking and getting to know each other. Sir Frolick never liked me. He wasn't mean to me, but I could tell Caycee was his favorite girl.

We left the cave, and Caycee promised she would be back to see him. He was elated! I told him I would be back, and he snarled his lips and rolled his eyes. I knew then he certainly did not enjoy my company. It was clear he favored my sister over me.

"See you soon, my golden dragon." Sir Frolick jumped around and the ground shook violently and rocks came hurling down. "Let's get out of here before we get smashed by a bolder," Caycee and I ran out of the cave into the snow and then slid under the archway. We were back and the weather was very nice.

*"Tell a weary soul your secrets and sadness will remain;*
*tell a trusted friend your heart's desires*
*and a true confidante you will gain."*
(Nobel Reszen)

CHAPTER 14

# A Time of Sorrow

# A Time of Sorrow

Caycee and the dragon became splendid friends. She would visit him often and take Patsy Rose with her. Possum had to stay back at the farm. She was jittery around other people. They laughed and had walks and talks getting to know each other for several months. It was our secret and Mum and Father knew nothing. I mean, they suspected something was going on, but they trusted their dear trustworthy children.

One morning, Mum made scones with bacon honey, Caycee's favorite, and called her out of bed. I was already up and working the farm. Caycee would not get out of bed. Mum went in to check on her. She opened the curtains. "Caycee, you are never going to get work done by sleeping in all day."

Caycee was still. Mum felt her head, and she was burning up with a high fever. Mum used wet, warm clothes on her forehead every couple of hours for a few days. Caycee would not eat anything nor would she get out of bed. She could talk, but what she spoke did not make any sense. She was delirious from the high fever.

Everyone in the village prayed for our family. People came by from church during the day and the evening. They even brought food for us and checked in on our family often. That is what family does, especially a church family. They always make sure everyone is okay.

Finally, after three days the fever would not break, and we were very concerned. Dr. Rainton arrived at our home carrying a black leather satchel and wearing a stethoscope around his neck.

"Come in, Doctor. She is in her room." Mum walked him to the bedroom where Caycee lay resting. He examined her eyes, throat and then he looked at her fingertips. They were changing colors. He pressed her fingertips gently. There was not much movement from her. He had never seen this before; he had only read about it in his training to become a doctor. He asked Mum a few questions, but he knew what was going on just from the examination, and told her, "I have some solemn news—news I am sure you are not expecting, I have seen this type of sickness, and sadly, it is incurable."

Mum fell to the ground wailing in disbelief. Father put his hand on her back. "What do you mean, sickness? Is my only daughter going to die?"

The doctor replied, "She may. I'm sorry, there is no cure. I am not telling you both to lose hope. Caycee is the first person I have ever seen with it. There is always a chance for faith, but I am a medical doctor. I can only tell you what I know. I will send word to other fellow doctors and ask if there is anything I can do. I am so sorry, Anna and Reilly. Don't lose hope!"

The doctor explained to Mum and Father what to do to keep her comfortable. He mentioned that her fever may go down, but it will spike back up. He asked for Mum to continue to place cloths on her forehead, and give her plenty of liquids by spoon if possible. This would help her stay hydrated. He gave Mum some medicine which she could give her to alleviate any pain.

Father went to see Reverend McBrady at the church. He needed someone to help him during this time. Mum was extremely sad. I never saw her that way before, nor had I ever seen her cry such a deep, sorrowful cry. It was heartbreaking, and I was left by myself, grieving and wondering what to do and how to deal with it all.

In life you don't have a book that explains how to react to every situation, but I was reminded that Professor Nobel's dictionary explained it perfectly. It was a **"hopeseecombles"** moment—*a moment when you feel utterly helpless, and your heart slowly loses hope.*

*"Hold on tight to hope and reach for the stars.*
*Your faith will help you discover who you truly are."*
(Nobel Reszen)

Chapter 15

# Hope While Waiting

# Hope While Waiting

Many weeks passed. Days turned into weeks and weeks turned into months. Caycee began to lose locks of red hair. It was becoming thin in certain spots, and this made her very sad. It was tough for her to accept at first, but she realized it was part of what she was going through. It broke my heart when I saw her examining her hair in the mirror. She didn't know that I was watching her from the hallway. She placed her hands through her hair, and then began to cry. I knew this was affecting her and our family tried to help, but sometimes you must go through things on your own, process them and it takes time.

Family and friends pitched in to help Mum by taking shifts to care for her needs. Over time Caycee became silent. She suffered with depression. Dylan stopped by daily to read Caycee a story, even though she rarely responded to him. Feeding her was a challenge. Sometimes she responded, but most of the time she would take a bite of food and stare off as if we were not even in the room.

It was hard for me to watch my sister suffering. I wished it was me that was miserable instead of Caycee. Our family took things one day at a time. We hoped as we waited and believed for a miracle during everything that was going on. There were times when I needed a break from it all, because it was too much to bear. I was only a child, and it was hard for me to process what was happening.

Mum suggested I take Patsy to the shore for treasure hunting. It was hard for me to leave Caycee, but Mum insisted, "Go. You need some Yipson time away. Go on, get some wind in your face." She was right, always right!

Early in the morning, I ventured to the beach with Patsy Rose. Patsy's nose was trained for hunting treasures. She could sniff them out in a matter of seconds, although sometimes she would inhale sand in her nose and have sneezing fits. There was nothing I could do but chuckle at her.

Patsy explored as I soaked in the ocean view. I love Evolone Hills with its deep blue oceans and white capped waves. I lived in a **"caresuffcangis"**— *a place of beauty; a rare paradise.* Some loath solitude. They are bothered by the peace and quiet. They feel bored if they don't have something to do. It all sounds like whining to me, and I prefer the whining of the sea rather than that hobblesquashdo. **"Hobblesquashdo"** meaning *insignificant garbage, worthless thoughts.*

"Psst, Psst." What is this I hear? "Psst. Psst." I spun around and there before me leaning against the stone archway, pretending to hide but not cleaver at all, was none other than the golden dragon. "Well, if it isn't Sir Frolick, the ferocious dragon of Evolone Hills. Respectfully Yipson, at your attention." I tipped my cap in a sarcastic fashion.

In a low whisper, he said, "Come over here." Patsy Rose froze and was completely silent for the first time in her doggy life. At first, I was not sure of this initial advance by Frolick. After all, he didn't favor me, I could tell. He loved my sister, but my curiosity caused me to go against my better judgment, and I followed him into the cave.

In my mind, I was thinking, "What if I become a pillar of gold? One fire-breathing moment and I'm toast!" I passed by the stones, and the ground turned from sand to a sheet of ice. I slid across the ice to the entrance of the dark cave, watching his golden tail sway back and forth.

"Where is Caycee?" He reminded me of how she promised to come back. "It's been weeks since I have seen her." There is so much more he wanted to tell her and show her.

I told him she was sick. He said, "Bring her to me. I must see her." I cannot, Sir Frolick. She cannot even get out of bed. She is dying. How will I bring her to you?"

Sir Frolick burped and a clear bubble came out of his mouth. He blew on the inside of the bubble and it filled with fire. He said, "Take this bubble to your sister. Place it above her head, and it will float over her body. When she rises from her bed in a few days, bring her to me."

I hid the fire bubble in my jacket. I was afraid that I might pop it. Sir Frolick read my mind. "You won't pop it. Don't worry." I looked back at him with a grin. After all, it wasn't every day I was in the presence of a golden dragon.

Meanwhile, the church members along with Reverend McBrady were praying for Caycee's healing. Day and night they held candlelight watches, waiting in faith for King Nissi to answer their requests. They believed He would heal her.

On my way back home, I passed by the church and overheard an elderly woman praying. "Dear King Nissi, bring a miracle to Caycee. Heal her body and send Your Spirit to comfort her and protect her from harm. May Your angels watch over her and her family. Heal her, dear King Nissi. Send her the Spirit's fire!"

I was afraid Mum would see the fire bubble, but it became like a vapor and was not visible to the human eye. I didn't say anything to my mum. She was sitting quietly in the living room. I headed directly to my bedroom. Caycee was swaying in bed. I opened my hands and the ball of fire appeared. Both of us watched in amazement and nothing happened. Then the fire began to breathe and swirl around Caycee's body. I watched in **"Stipple-magnotion"** meaning *amazement and absolute wonder of the mind*. Sparks of fire ignited from the bubble and fell like rain. This fire was supernatural, and her body was not burned. It was refined in a way that is hard to explain.

Caycee fell back into a deep sleep, and the fire dissipated and disappeared.

I anxiously waited for a few days, checking on Caycee more than I ever had. It happened just as Sir Frolick said. Caycee awoke. She sat up and wanted to eat something other than soup! Mum came running into the room. She screamed in excitement and Father hugged her. Caycee was back. She sat up and she felt energy. A smile beamed on her face. Our family was so grateful for prayer. King Nissi answered our prayers, and He used a fire-breathing dragon to do it.

Over time Caycee's hair began to slowly grow back. Dr. Rainton came to the house to examine her, and he was amazed at her progress. He thought she was going to die, but it was clear: A miraculous healing was in process.

There is always hope for every situation. Caycee grew stronger, but still needed time to rest. After all, her body was healing and healing takes time. Caycee became frustrated at the process of healing. She wanted to do more than she physically could. Every time she pushed it, she ended up paying for it in some aggravating way.

For instance, she was tired of being in bed, but her legs were still weak. She decided to get out of bed, not listening to Mum, and walked over to the dresser, lost her balance, fell on the ground and bruised her arm. Regardless of her stubbornness, Mum rushed to her side to see if she was okay. "Caycee, give it time. You'll be running before you know it. Don't give up. There is hope."

"In life everyone should wait for their turn. In time your turn will come. Try to be patient," Mum said sincerely. Caycee sighed. She knew Mum was right, but it didn't make it any easier for her while waiting

*"Be patient in wisdom and wait to take your turn,*
*for if you refuse to give matters their proper time,*
*then an unpleasant lesson you will miserably learn."*
(Nobel Reszen).

CHAPTER 16

# A Grand Celebration

# A Grand Celebration

Lord Gregory and his son Dylan were ready to brave the mighty ocean. Dylan couldn't leave without saying good-bye to Caycee. After all, she was his close friend. He cared for her deeply. He loved her.

I reminded Caycee of how Dylan was by her side day in and day out reading her stories and praying for her. He had an unshakable faith. Caycee didn't remember him being there because she was so sick, but she wanted to thank him in person before his father, Lord Gregory, sailed away.

Mum decided that we should have the grandest celebration. After all, the prayers of the faithful were answered and Caycee was healed. Mum contacted all the women and local businesses. This was going to be a grand event. Lord Gregory decided to stay a few more days, and Madam Mamsie was elated! She loved her sea captain.

Mum spun Caycee a beautiful dress out of fine ivory linen. She stitched tiny white flowers gingerly throughout. Father was assigned to solder a one-of-a-kind metal cage for underneath. This would give the dress the fullness it needed. Caycee was self-conscious about her hair. It was not as thick like before. Mum wrapped a headband in green ivy strands to place on her head. Caycee absolutely loved it! She twirled in front of the oval mirror, and her eyes were aglow.

Everyone gathered by the shore for this grand celebration. There, under the lights, Dylan asked Caycee for the first dance. It was a dance of victory, and he dressed for the occasion. He had metal armor, and for this enchanted moment, he wore a white and grey screened fencing helmet.

"My lady," he stepped towards her as the orchestra played in the background and as whimsical paper mache stars twinkled in the trees. I even think I saw a few BobbyBugglebees gently swaying as well. As they danced, the sea became choppy as the sky filled with lightning.

My sister was healed, she was going to live and it was the best day of my life. Our prayers had been answered. Soon I realized this was no storm but something else. The ground shook beneath me and before the assembly of others stood a mighty angel. He was over ten feet high—higher than a grizzly bear standing on his tiptoes. He had eyes of fire and a blinding light that shined from his wings. Mum and Father had seen him before they escaped from the evil King Ballot. They were not afraid. Many panicked, some ran away fleeing to the mountains while others jumped into the sea. I, Yipson Minor, was unafraid. So were my mum or father and Reverend McBrady.

Now Dylan's hair managed to fall out of his helmet. That was quite humorous! You cannot hold curly hair down. Long ago, it was prophesied to King Ballot that his curse could be removed. "There is only One to break the curse upon your head and the locks of her hair are red," the angel said.

"We honor you today, Caycee Minor, for you have been brave, you have believed and you have remained strong. King Nissi has answered the prayers others prayed for you, and you have been healed."

Meanwhile at the kingdom, King Ballot's emotional chains were broken, and he began to gain weight. The kingdom began to flourish again, and he felt awful for the way he had treated the people. King Ballot decided to give his castle to the people, and he and his queen lived in the swamp below. He wanted to see firsthand what he put them through. It was miserable conditions, but he was truly happy for his heart became generous again.

"Dragon, come forth," he shouted! Out from the cave flew Sir Frolick. He swerved underneath the stone arches and swooped down directly in front of Caycee. He rose above her head and clapped his wings together. Gold dust fell all around her and flocking her linen dress. She looked beautiful covered in golden glitter, a royal golden princess indeed.

*"Gold glitters and it shines,*
*but only a soul healed by the Spirit can truly be refined."*
(Nobel Reszen)

Chapter 17

# Fight and Remain

# Fight and Remain

As Professor Nobel's dictionary states, "**Warrior-right-on**," which means *an individual who remains faithful to fight in any situation, knowing that their inner strength comes from within.*"

It was hard for my parents to remain in an evil kingdom, but while they did, they made provision to leave and soon freedom came. It was hard for us as a family to remain when Patsy Rose was injured and we had a choice of life or death. Life may be different, but we chose life. It was hard to remain when Caycee became sick.

In life, many things may come. Some of those things are good and bring us extraordinary joy. Some are not and bring us great sorrow. Whatever comes our way, it is important that we remain positive, remain steadfast and believe with continued hope as we stand and fight for the ones we love, even when we feel like we don't have enough strength to go any further.

Often people asked, "What if your sister dies? What if she does not get the healing you are praying for?" I wish I could answer that question simply. However, the body may die, but the spirit and soul of the person live on forever. Each one of us has a spirit and a soul. It can be difficult to understand this because we are mortal. My reasoning is that it is important to have faith and believe one may be healed, even if the healing never comes the way one expects.

When too many things cloud my mind, I often find writing is a way to put things in perspective. I find my solace near the ocean, and one day I wrote a song while watching the waves flood into the shore and the gentle breeze kiss my face. The smell of salt and fish was in the air, but my heart was troubled and I felt despair. So I raised my pen and began to sing, and hope began to rise within me. My faith was strengthened and my heart was glad. I became extremely grateful and thanked King Nissi for everything I had.

I was not alone that day on the shore for a great crowd of Minnyboasters surrounded me, helping me sing the song I titled "Remain."

**Verse 1**
In life we must remain
through sorrow and through pain.
We may never understand the why's.
We will find our strength,
and faith will be our friend,
and we won't dare give in to foolish pride.

### Chorus

*No matter what life brings*
*We will stand and we will sing*
*for our life is worth the fight to remain.*

*No power in heav'n nor earth*
*Will ever change our worth,*
*for our life is worth the fight to remain.*

### Verse 2

No more sorrow will there be,
only love and liberty.
We will rise with angels' wings and fly

### Verse 3

All our pain will disappear
as our Savior draws us near.
There will be no sorrow or tears.

### Chorus

*No more sorrow will there be,*
*only love and liberty.*
*We will soar eternally and we will, Remain.*

There is freedom deep in the heart of each one of us, and I am reminded of a song I grew up singing with my family. A song of freedom: "One day when the winds are blowin' and the moon's light is showin', we'll be knowin', freedom is ours. We'll be lights on the ocean, free from commotion, and we'll hold tight to each other knowin', freedom is ours."

The kingdom was restored and Caycee was ultimately healed from her illness. Everyone displayed

**"Gloryburt'ims"** meaning *extremely happy and joyful outbursts rendering thanksgiving.* However, the story doesn't end there, and my friends, that of course is for a **"Bafflateoplious"** meaning *another time.*

## AN IRISH BLESSING FOR YOU!

How could I end this book, without sending you off with a wish from my heart? So I give you an Irish Blessing from the hills of Evolone, for I believe that is the finest way to start.

May you rest ever so peacefully under the shadow of a four-leaf clover. May you rise to be courageous never fearing what lies ahead; may you always make time for a good cup of tea with a trusted friend, and may your belly be filled with a warm slice of Irish bread.

May you be happy and find comfort, even when your heart is sad. May you always find the treasure in the good times and in the bad. May you rise to be all you were created to be; may you always seek the King in times of utter joy and fear in the uncertainties.

May you grow in your faith and rise above; and may you know that no matter what happens in this life, you are dearly loved. May the sun shine upon your face and touch you with everlasting grace, and may you never forget you are more than the circumstances which you face.

*"Sometimes the end is where you must begin.*
*Never give up and never give in,*
*for although time will not necessarily bend,*
*if you continually fight,*
*faith and persistence will enviably win."*
(Nobel Reszen)

# About the Author

Holly Szurpicki was born in Detroit, Michigan, the car capital of the world. Although she couldn't drive yet, her imagination had a way of taking her wherever she dreamed to go.

Holly wished one day to be a princess, a park ranger, or an entrepreneur. She states, "Two out of three is not too shabby."

She is passionate about creating stories, screenplays and writing songs. Holly began writing a manuscript in the year 2001 which laid dormant. Holly focused in on raising her two children and when the year 2008 arrived, she teamed up with a virtual animation studio out of New York. That is when the dream came to life, and the Shorty Bean story became her first novel.

Art and individual creativity have tremendously inspired her throughout her career. Holly possesses visual creativity which takes her to places beyond words to live animation in her mind. Being able to envision her characters and their environments is a true gift, and she recognizes this as supernatural.

Despite many tragic circumstances she has faced throughout her life, Holly always maintains a positive attitude and loves to encourage others to pursue their God-given dreams.

Her goal for writing children's books is to create a safe and wholesome environment for imagination. Holly desires for children to DREAM BIG, and never forget that there is nothing impossible with God. She believes each one of us has a divine destiny and wants others to never be afraid to pursue their dreams.

Holly lives in northern Minnesota with her husband and two children and a water dog named Klause. She loves the outdoors, photography and fishing to name a few of her passions.

For more information regarding the Shorty Bean series, future works or general inquiries, check out her website: www.hollykszurpicki.com